Eli's Night-Light

Eli's Night-Light

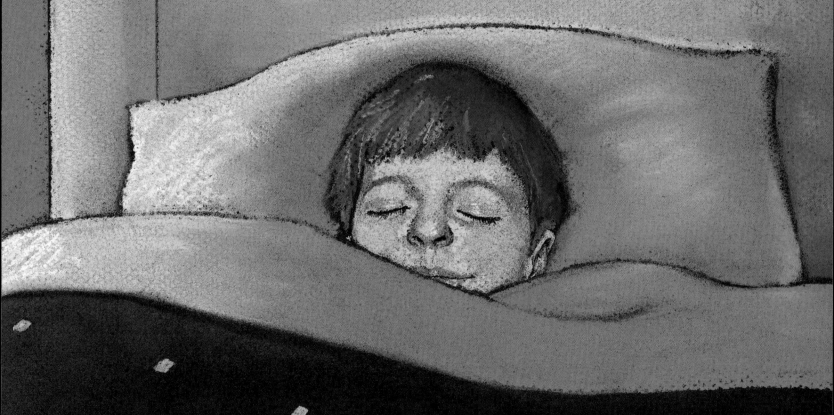

by LIZ ROSENBERG

illustrated by JOANNA YARDLEY

ORCHARD BOOKS   NEW YORK
An Imprint of Scholastic Inc.

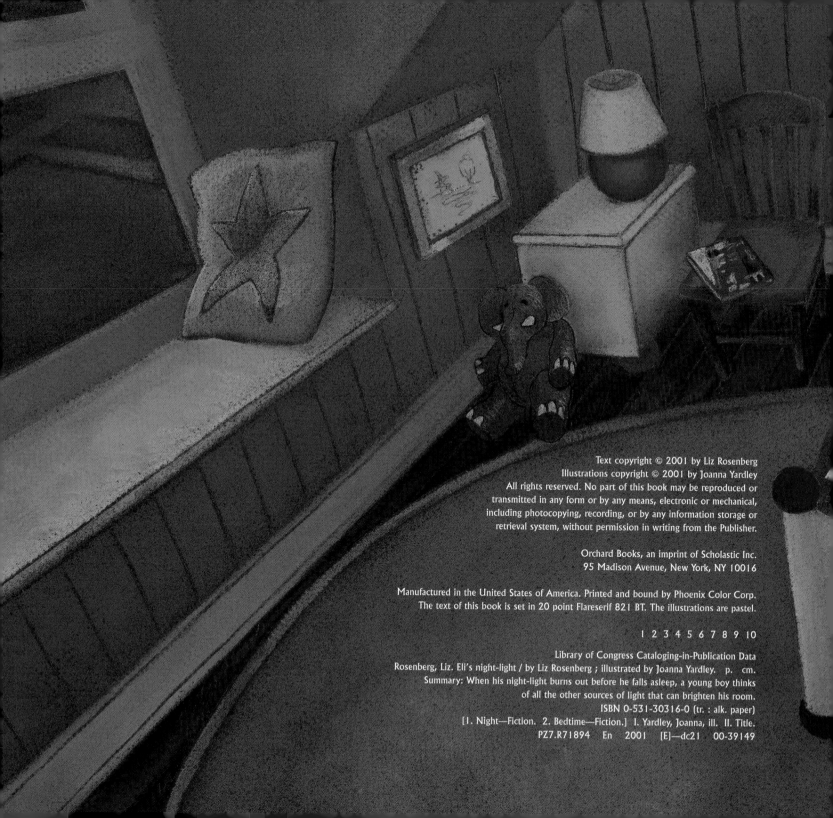

Orchard Books, an imprint of Scholastic Inc.
95 Madison Avenue, New York, NY 10016

Manufactured in the United States of America. Printed and bound by Phoenix Color Corp.
The text of this book is set in 20 point Flareserif 821 BT. The illustrations are pastel.

1 2 3 4 5 6 7 8 9 10

Library of Congress Cataloging-in-Publication Data
Rosenberg, Liz. Eli's night-light / by Liz Rosenberg ; illustrated by Joanna Yardley.   p.   cm.
Summary: When his night-light burns out before he falls asleep, a young boy thinks
of all the other sources of light that can brighten his room.
ISBN 0-531-30316-0 (tr. : alk. paper)
[1. Night—Fiction. 2. Bedtime—Fiction.] I. Yardley, Joanna, ill. II. Title.
PZ7.R71894 En 2001 [E]—dc21 00-39149

For Eli, absolutely forever—
and as usual. Love, Mom.
—L.M.R.

For the mighty Quinn
—J.Y.

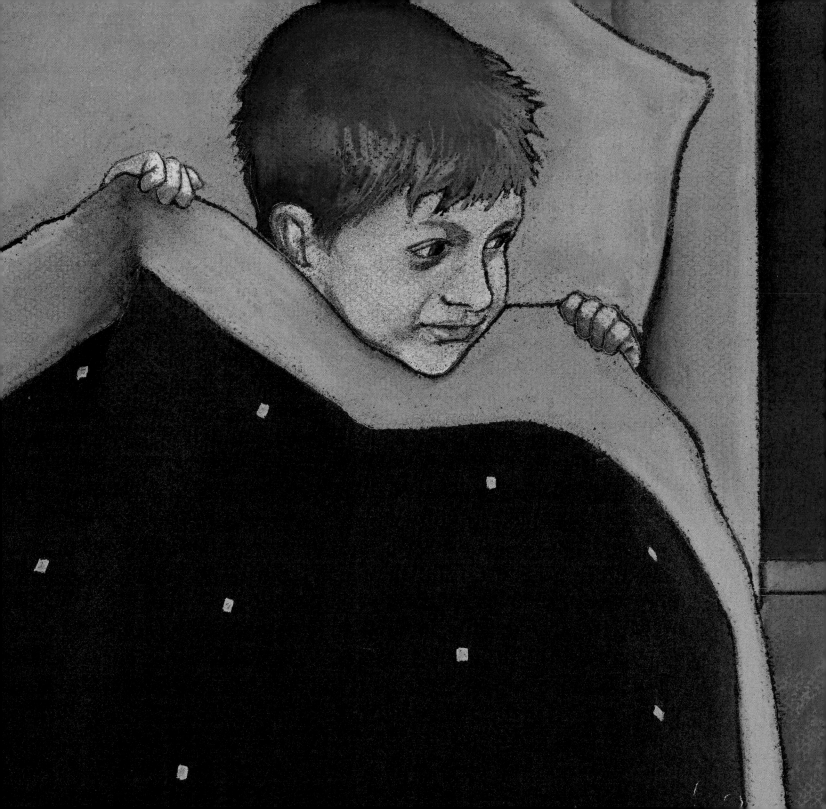

*E*li's night-light burned out one night
just before he could fall asleep.
He thought, *It's too late to wake up my mother and father.*

All the dark in his room grew larger.
He said, "What else can be my night-light tonight?"
His bed was as black as a piece of coal.
His closet yawned like a dragon's hole. . . .

Then he saw a small gleam
from the crack at the door.
It made a shining dent in the dark.

His clock glowed red on the chest of drawers.

Headlights splashed one side of the wall
and fell in a patch on his soccer ball.

The stripes of his wallpaper shone in the dark,
and so did the frame on his picture of the park.

Out in the street a light blinked red,
throwing bright circles above the bed.

Eli peeked out.

Above his head—
above his house—

above the world—

shone hundreds of stars that would not
burn out for a long, long time.

He said, "These can be
my night-light tonight—

and on any night when
I need something bright."

Then he fell asleep, and slept all night
in the dark and the light.
Like you did—just last night.

Good night, good night.